The ADVENTURES of
DUCK POO
ISLAND

Jizammie J. Griggs

PAGE PUBLISHING, INC.
New York, NY

First originally published by Page Publishing, Inc. 2015

ISBN 978-1-68213-192-3 (pbk)
ISBN 978-1-68213-193-0 (digital)

Printed in the United States of America

This book is dedicated to Mrs. Evelyn Allen, my favorite teacher who believed in me enough to have me read Langston Hughes, during class, Mrs. Allen I don't know if you know this or not but it changed my life, thank you for believing in me.
And forcing others to give me a chance. (Basketball)

This book is dedicated to my mom and best friend Mrs. Alice M. Griggs, thanks for instilling in me your strength and tenacity The way you took on Atlanta by yourself and raised two kids and made the tough decisions to get us out of there when you did, well I'm just grateful, I truly admire you, thanks Ma.

Friendship is born at that moment when one person says to another: 'What! You too?' I thought I was the only one.

—C.S. Lewis

A friend is one that knows you as you are, understands where you have been, accepts what you have become, and still, gently allows you to grow.

—William Shakespheare

In the beginning there were countless stories of the mysterious island that absolutely everyone was scared to visit because of the tales about visitors who never returned. Also the strange sounds and eyewitness accounts of ghosts dressed in all white, singing a gleeful but spooky melody that to the listeners made their skin crawl. The stories go as far back as the nineteenth century, but our story starts in the present day, in a small town called Green Lake. It is the story of four unsuspecting heroes who will soon change their town and reveal the mysteries of Duck Poo Island.

CHAPTER 1

HOMECOMING

As our story begins, it is homecoming. The Green Lake Ducks had just won their game against crosstown rival Shoreline Badgers. Oh yes, this is a very exciting time in Green Lake. There were barbecues, parades, exciting people, returning alumni, and of course, the media. Football is very big in Mallard County or, as the people of Green Lake would call it, Duck Country, but the Shoreline Badgers would be opposed to calling Mallard County Duck Country. You see, these are two small towns, and they both use the football stadium, built with shared money between the two towns. So this rivalry game was more than just a notch in the winners and losers column. This county is divided between Ducks and Badgers, and for the last five years straight, the Ducks had claimed the homecoming title. And yes, I am just the narrator, but if you asked me, the Ducks had earned the right to call this county Duck Country because, as you know, in any rivalry, the winner earns bragging rights. But that's just my two cents. Now back to the story. It is now Sunday, and the streets are abuzz with families, vendors, and exciting sounds and smells. Now this is where the story really picks up.

Here is Andy and he is with his best friend Adam. They both attend Mallard County Middle School. There is only one middle school in the county, and both Shoreline and Green Lake kids attended Mallard County Middle School. So yes, the Ducks and the Badgers are very familiar with each other. After eighth grade graduation, it would seem like there's a choice of which high school one will go to between Line High and Lake High. But this decision has traditionally been stripped away from the kids and predicated on which school their parents went to, and yes, sometimes there is a mother and a father who happened to crossbreed their offspring. Then usually, the father, being more active in sports and probably played football for one of the high schools, gets to make the final decision, normally without opposition. So at the eighth grade graduation, kids who have been friends since kindergarten instantaneously become rivals, and this plays out for the rest of their lives through friendships, networking, business, even job opportunities. Make no mistake about it. Mallard County is definitely divided as clearly as two rival street gangs screaming, "What set you claiming!" In this situation, it is Shoreline or Green Lake, Badger or Duck, the Brown and Gold, or the Green and Black. Eighth grade graduation is a huge defining moment for Mallard County.

After graduation, some families move clean across town, which is a clear signal as to where their loyalty lies. Andy and Adam are at this point, and after this year, their friendship will be tested, challenged, threatened even. But they have vowed to stay best friends no matter what. They will definitely part ways due to the fact that Adam's Dad was a Badger and Andy's Dad was a Duck.

As we join Andy and Adam at the lake, they're enjoying the festive smells and sounds that surround them.

Andy said, "You smell that, Adam?"

Adam said, "Yes, that smells like Uncle Ken's teriyaki house."

"No, not that," said Andy as the area was very saturated with the aroma of Peking duck.

"Andy," said Adam, "I smell teriyaki, peaking duck to be more specific. And why does Uncle Ken call it peaking duck anyways? Is the duck sticking its head out of the pot while he's cooking it?"

"No, Adam," said Andy. "Not peaking duck. It's Peking duck."

"Well! What does that mean?" asked Adam.

"I don't know," said Andy. "It has to do with the Orient or something. It's an Asian thing. Anyways, Adam, not that smell. Smell again. This time open your mouth a little. Can't you smell that hint of confection that flows ever so softly through the nostrils and down on to your palate?"

"Onto my what?" asked Adam.

"Your palate," said Andy. "It's your tongue. Can't you almost taste it?"

"No, I can't taste anything," said Adam. "But I'll tell you what. I am never tasting again. And that's Uncle Ken's Peking duck. He can call it whatever he wants to call it, I know those are the same ducks from out here in this lake and I'd bet the championship on that."

"It's cotton candy," said Andy, referring to the sweet smell that Adam just couldn't smell.

"Hello, boys," said Anne, who is Andy's big sister. She was the head cheerleader at Lake High. That's right. She's a Duck, and she loves to boss her little brother and his friends around. "What cha doing?" asked Anne.

"Nothing," said the boys. "Don't you have a beauty pageant or a miniskirt contest to get to?" asked Andy in his most transparent "get lost" tone ever.

"Yes, I do," said Anne. "But it's not until twelve o'clock, and it is only ten o'clock so that gives me two hours to watch you like Mom said."

"Well!" said Andy, "Adam and I are about to go pedal boating."

"No, you are not," said Anne. "My pageant is in two hours, and I am not going to spend the next hour and a half looking for you. Mom said she will meet us there, so for the next hour and a half, you're stuck with me."

"No way, Anne," said Andy. "We are going to catch fish to sell to Uncle Ken."

"Don't you mean ducks," said Adam. They laughed.

"Laugh all you want," said Anne, "but if you go fishing, I'm coming too."

"Oh, now I smell it," said Adam. "Cotton candy, right?"

"Cool," said Andy. "Let's get a bag for the ride."

As they gathered their things and went to the vendor to buy a bag of cotton candy, they ran into Adam's big brother, Jay, who had been looking all over for Adam.

"There you go, you little rug rat, come here," said Jay as he grabbed Adam.

Adam yelled, "Let me go," as he endured noogies accompanied with wet willies that smelled like root beer floats.

"Leave him alone, you big bully," said Anne. "Pick on someone your own size like a Green Lake High football player."

Laughter ensued due to the fact that Jay was a Badger. Not to mention, the starting quarterback for the Shoreline High School Badgers. That's right, the alpha dog to a half a county full of lamenting Badgers. Trust me, if you were there, you would have laughed too. Even Adam joined in but couldn't deny that part of him was definitely conflicted because he was destined to be on the side of the Badgers. As Andy paid for his cotton candy, they selected a pedal boat.

Jay asked, "Where do you guys think you're going? I just found you, and Dad will kill me if I lose you again. We're going fishing."

"You can come too," said Andy.

"No," said Adam and Anne simultaneously.

"I mean we just don't need any more extra deadweight," said Anne. "Because if the boat tipped over and I ruin my dress, my mom would have a conniption. I would have a conniption."

"Andy, what's a conniption?" asked Adam.

"Anne is a conniption," said Andy.

"Okay, I have it, guys," said Jay. "We'll take two boats. That way, Anne doesn't have to worry about getting her little tiara wet, and I can also keep an eye on you. You're riding with me, Adam."

"Okay," exclaimed Adam. "Let's just go already."

"Oh great! Now I'm stuck with Anne and her girly scarf," said Andy. "You see, Anne liked to tie a scarf around the hand post. I guess for good luck. Call it superstitious or maybe just a girl thing. Who knows."

CHAPTER 2

THE ISLAND

As the two pairs of siblings head down to the shore they continued quarreling, and no one looks up to notice the storm approaching in the distance.

Meanwhile, back in town, Sheriff Jacoby Adam and Jay's dad is inundated with reports of break-ins and thefts. While people were out enjoying the festivities, criminals were taking advantage of the situation by helping themselves to the citizen's belongings.

Back at the lake, Andy and Adam are having a really good day. So much so Anne decided to join in just as long as she didn't have to bait her own hook.

"Help me, Andy!" said Anne. "Put it on the hook."

"You do it yourself," said Andy. "It can't hurt you."

"I know," said Anne. "But it's so slimy."

"Okay, Anne, let me help you," said Jay. Side note: Anne and Jay have a history. Back in middle school, Anne had a huge crush on Jay. They went to the eighth grade graduation; danced together, but after that; they parted ways and now act as if they barely even know each other.

"We better head back soon," said Anne. "It's already eleven fif-teen, and it's starting to get dark."

"Yeah, I think Anne is right," said Jay.

"Just one more fish," said Andy.

"No," said Anne. "It's time to go. The wind is picking up, and it's getting dark. It's about to storm. Time to go, guys."

All of a sudden, it began to rain heavily. The clouds were dark, and the wind began to howl.

"Oh no," said Anne. "My hair is a mess, my dress is ruined. Mom is going to kill me."

Suddenly, the boats began to float apart. Adam yelled for Andy as Andy yelled Adam's name as well. They pedaled toward each other but to no avail. The winds had separated them and sent them hurling far out into the water. Jay tried to gain control of the boat by pedal-ing hard, but the waves were too strong. Jay tried to grab and hold Adam, but Adam slipped and fell off the boat into the cold, rampag-ing water. Jay screamed, "Adam!"

Adam yelled, "Help! Help me!" But Adam's plea for help quickly became faint as the storm raged.

With no signs of help around, it was not looking good for them. Jay had lost Adam to the rapids and could no longer see Anne and Andy's boat. Jay was all alone so he cried. That's right, Jay cried for losing Adam, for being trapped in the boat during this storm, but he also cried because he felt as if he was the reason why his dad didn't come to the lake. He thought that his dad was ashamed of him for losing the homecoming game. Little did Jay know his dad had challenges of his own, trying to manage the town's problems with incoming calls of theft and the natural disasters caused by the storm like power lines being down, fallen trees lying in the middle of the road, traffic accidents, and on top of all of these, Sheriff Jacoby was having no luck reaching his boys by phone.

As the storm started to subside and the sun slowly began to peek through the heavy, thick clouds, Anne began to awaken. She and Andy were floating about seventeen kilometers down lake, about two kilometers away from the no-name island. This island had been notorious for tales of witchcraft, hauntings, and the island was even blamed for claiming the souls of the local kids who had ran away to the island, never to be seen again.

As Anne awoke, she groggily called out to Andy, "Andy, wake up. Wake up, Andy. Are you okay? Where are we?"

As Andy struggled to orientate himself with his surroundings, his watery eyes cleared as he raised his head up. He muttered, "The island. Look, Anne, the island."

This was very different for the kids of Green Lake. You see, although the kids had grown up there and seen the island every clear day, they were forbidden to travel out to the island. The grownups even told them that the island was an old military mine testing site, and that the kids should steer clear of it. This was one of those justifiable lies that adults convince themselves was necessary to keep order and peace. It must not be a sin if you can justify it. Justifiable sins—never seen that book in the King James Version. It must be in one of those lost books of the Bible. Well, for the most part, it seemed to have worked although it was thought that the reported kids who ran away set up on the island, and there are stories of a forming vagabond society, but this was dismissed and thought to have no validity to it.

With the sun shining brightly now, it is almost as though the storm never happened. As Anne and Andy reached the beach of the island, they noticed that there were tribal-type boats that were already there. This was peculiar due to the fact that they were told no one ever came to the island. Andy immediately became suspicious and told Anne to be quiet and to get down.

On the island, there was a cave, and the water traveled through the mouth of the cave. An eerie sight, it looked as if the island was eating the water. Suddenly, two figures appeared at the mouth's opening, but there was a glare from the sun shining off the water that impaired their sight.

"Who is that?" asked Anne, not really expecting a response. "What are they doing?"

"I'm not sure," Andy whispered as he listened to see if he could pick up their conversation. "Shhh," said Andy, "listen."

Both men were very sketchy; they appeared to be in their forties, and both men had walkie-talkies and earpieces as if they were secretly communicating with others. One man had an eyepatch and a scruffy beard, the other was bald and had a whip at his waist as if he was preparing to tame lions or something. But these guys were not part of some island-style Barnum and Bailey act. These guys are true-to-life pirates, bad guys committed to live by the sea and die by the sea.

At this point, Anne and Andy could tell that something just wasn't right. As they eavesdropped on the pirates' conversation, they kept hearing the word emerald mentioned over and over again. "Is there more emeralds?" "Can we get more emeralds?" "We need more emeralds"—this was the conversation of the pirates with the background music of drilling and moaning. "Do you hear that Anne?," said Andy. "It sounds like people moaning, and there's drilling? Do you think the pirates are drilling for gold?"

"Yes," said Anne, "but that's hard work. It must be more than just the two. We have to be careful."

"I know," said Andy. "But what can we do? We can't just stay here! How will we get home?" There was silence, for Anne had no answers to Andy's barrage of questions. "We have to get closer," Andy said.

"No, Andy. We need to leave," Anne nervously muttered. "I'm scared. We need to just turn around and get back into our boat and leave." As these words shuddered out of Anne's mouth, she turned around to view the boat, and to her surprise, it had drifted surprisingly far away from the shore, and there was no chance of them retrieving this vessel. "Oh no! What will we do now?" asked Anne. "What about your cell phone?" Andy inquired. "Does it work?"

"No," said Anne.

"Well now, we must get closer," explained Andy to see if there's some sort of communication device to radio for help. "Stay low and quiet."

As Anne and Andy braved the unknown hazards of the island, Jay was floating only a few minutes away from the island but on the opposite side. Jay started to pedal back towards mainland in hopes of seeing Adam floating on some God-sent piece of buoyant debris when he spotted Anne and Andy's pedal boat floating with no signs of Anne or Andy on board. Although there were other stranded pedal boats adrift around him, he specifically noticed this one because of the scarf Anne tied around the hand post. At that point, Jay figured that either they were dead or they swam to the island. So Jay began pedaling as fast as he could muster to the beach of the island in hopes of finding Anne, Andy, and especially Adam, safe and sound together on the beach around a fire, roasting sea fish and crab. And although this seemed farfetched and very unlikely all rolled into one, sometimes when the chips are down, all you need is a little hope and a lot of psychotic imagery to spur you on headfirst into an open hand slap of reality. And no, there may not be a fire waiting for Jay, no sea fish and crab. Just to find his fellow travelers safe and together would have been worth the delusional burst of energy that he needed to get him through his moment of emotional breakdown at sea.

As Jay finally reached the island, he heard the drilling and moaning sounds. This surprised Jay since he knew no one ever came to the island, so in his mind, he thought it had to be Anne or Andy, and it sounded as if they were wounded. So Jay rushed up the slack hill, restraining himself from calling out, just in case his assumptions were incorrect, and the sounds were not made by his fellow travelers.

As Jay reached the apex of the hill, he spotted movement. He could see the mouth of the cave, and at the edge, there were two tall figures manhandling a smaller figure as if they were cops arresting a bad guy. The smaller person being handled had a bag on his head, the kind of bag that you would fill with potatoes. The kind of bag that was more of a sack made from spun wool or some type of course yarn that definitely had to be the most itchy fiber ever manufactured on God's green earth. This made Jay feel for the apprehended individual, not just for being roughed up and captured but for what Jay could imagine this person must be going through having that sack on, being pushed around, working up a sweat, having those itchy loose fibers stick to his sweaty skin creating a suffocating itch that can only be described as torturous.

Clearly Jay needed to investigate to find out what was really going on. As Jay inched closer, he started to recognize facial features. He recognized one of the men from a wanted poster in the Sheriff's office, but what were they doing on this island. Suddenly, a much larger man appeared and began to argue with the first two. Roughly, they begin to remove the bag from the apprehended individual's head. To Jay's astonishment, it was Adam. Glory to the most high. This made Jay feel very perplexed. You see, on the one hand, Adam was okay. He wasn't fish food or some unlikely victim to Davy Jones's locker. But on the other hand, Adam was in danger, and Jay had no clue as to how he was going to rescue him.

Meanwhile, on the other side of the island, Anne and Andy had managed to creep closer and not be seen. Thanks to Andy's Boy Scout background, they were capable of maneuvering the terrain while remaining incognito.

"Look, Anne," said Andy as the pirates removed the bag from Adam's head. "It's Adam, and the pirates have him."

"No way," said Anne. "Do you see, Jay?"

"No," said Andy, "but we have to rescue Adam."

"As Andy started to move forward," Anne yelled. "Wait, we can't do this alone, not against those pirates. We have no weapons, no communications, and our pedal boat has a mind of its own. We can't just storm down there and throw a hissy fit demanding that they release Adam." "I know," said Andy. "But I have to do something. If it was vice versa he would do something for me. I know said Anne, we need help."

All of a sudden, from the right side of the brush, they could hear footsteps. Andy told Anne to grab something anything. Andy had a stick, and Anne begin picking up rocks that were close to her feet. As this strange silhouette moved closer, Anne began to pelt it with rocks. As Andy swung his big stick, he connected with this unknown person, right in the midsection, causing this person to gasp for air while saying, "Stop, Anne. Stop, Andy. It's me Jay."

Anne and Andy were so happy to see Jay. They ran over to hug his aching body, creating additional pain by squeezing his bruised torso.

Jay said, "They have Adam."

"I know," said Andy "we have to help him." "Yes," said Jay, "but we need a plan. First thing we need to do is get closer to see what is going on inside the cave."

"I know," said Anne. The drilling and moaning from the cave has been continuous. "I know," said Jay. "We may have to rescue more than just Adam. Let me go," said Andy. "I'm small, and I can get closer to the cave without being seen."

"No, Andy," said Anne. "Stay back. Let Jay or myself go. You'll only get caught, and they will have you and Adam both."

"No, they won't," said Andy. "I got us both this far."

"No," said Anne as Jay interrupted Anne and Andy's annoying impasse.

"Andy's right, Anne. The trees turn into small bushes the closer you get to the mouth of the cave, and Andy's the only one that can move in this area without being spotted."

After Andy and Jay finally convinced Anne to let Andy go, Andy made his way down the slippery hill and across the field of bushes to the cave. He managed to enter the cave without incident. He stayed low and alongside the caves wall, which was lined with equipment and heavy machinery. Andy could hear voices coming from about twenty yards deep into the cave. As Andy cautiously approached, he could see a cluster of men in the middle of the cave, and a little way back, he could see others. By the tone of the voices in conversation, Andy could tell who was in charge. The bigger guy was in charge, the one with the eyepatch and the long, greasy hair. He had a very deep but loud voice, and Andy heard the others call him cap, which had to be short for Captain, which meant that they were pirates and, therefore, very dangerous.

CHAPTER 3

THE CAVE

As Andy was doing his best to eavesdrop on the pirates' conversation so that he could gain as much information as possible, he accidentally kicked an oil pan that was underneath one of the vehicles. The Captain asked, "What was that?" As they all looked toward the entrance of the cave, "Go check it out," said the Captain. Quickly, the pirates scurried toward the vehicles, but Andy was ghost. He had managed to crawl under one of the vehicles and lifted himself up and out of sight. Very close call, but Andy wasn't out of harm's way yet as he heard one of the pirates say "All clear, Captain." The engine started in the vehicle that Andy was under. It began moving deeper and deeper into the cave while Andy did his best to hold on for dear life.

It took about twenty minutes for the pirate to finally park the vehicle, which for Andy felt more like an hour. When Andy finally felt that the coast was clear, he crawled from under the vehicle and looked around to view what can only be described as a nightmare.

He saw about twenty people alongside the wall with chains connecting them together. The pirates were forcing them to work, to dig for something, and the majority of them were kids ranging from twelve to seventeen years old. They all looked very tired, and some of them were hurt. That explained the moaning that he and Anne heard earlier. Suddenly, Andy heard a faint voice coming from the shadows along the wall of the cave. He reared upward to get a better view, then he heard that voice a second time, but he could barely make out what it was saying. So Andy rose up even more. Peering into the darkness, he still could not make out who that was or what they were saying. He needed to come from under the vehicle to obtain a better vantage point. All of a sudden, a loud voice screamed, "Stay down." It was Adam, and although Andy could not see him, he recognized his voice.

Very hurriedly, a pirate jumped down from the very vehicle that Andy was under, startling him. "Quiet down, you maggots," said the pirate, "and keep picking away at that wall. And that goes double for you, newcomer. The Captain don't care that your daddy is the law. We make the law around here. I got my eye on you," said the pirate with an eyepatch covering his left eye. "A zinger. That might have been funny under different circumstances." But Adam could tell that the pirate meant business. "So," said the pirate, "anymore noise out of you, and it's off to the gallows for you."

As the pirate slowly walked away, whistling, the kid chained next to Adam asked, "Is Sheriff Jacoby your dad?"

"Yes," said Adam, "and he's going to rescue us. All of us. What's your name?"

"My name is Toby. And yours?"

"My name is Adam, Adam Jacoby." "Well, Adam Jacoby, I wouldn't hold my breath if I were you." Said Toby. My girlfriend and I have been on this island digging up emeralds for these pirates for almost a year now."

"That long?," said Adam.

"Yes," said Toby. "I once saw a newspaper that one of the pirates accidentally left behind. And it read that my girlfriend and I had run off together to elope. They speculated that we went to Las Vegas."

"Las Vegas?" asked Adam.

"Yeah," said Toby. "I guess it's supposed to be easy to get married in Vegas, but you see, I don't even think they're looking for us anymore."

"But they are," said Adam. "You see, that kid over there under the truck? That's Andy. He's my best friend, and if I was to go to Vegas to get married, he'd be my best man. He's going to rescue us. I just know it."

"A little kid like that?" asked Toby. "Him and what army?"

"Oh no!" said Adam. "Don't underestimate Andy. He's very resourceful. I'm sure he'll figure something out."

"Well," said Toby, "he better have a good plan. The last guy that tried to escape hasn't been seen for weeks."

"Weeks?" asked Adam. "What, did they kill him?"

"No," said Toby. "Worse. For trying to escape, they put him on poo detail."

"What's that?" asked Adam.

Toby explained, "He has to collect duck poo. Haven't you noticed since you arrived to this island that there is duck poo everywhere? They combined it with the natural phosphorus that is in the cave's walls, and it creates an acid base isotope that eats away at the cave's walls, making it easier to drill."

"What is phosphorus?" asked Adam.

"Guess," said Toby, obviously upset. "It's all this white stuff that we're covered in every stinking day. It covers everything. You know, a couple years back, we were speedboating pass this island, and I could've sworn that I saw a younger girl dressed in all white along the shore of the island. She looked ghostly. I was scared to tell anyone because I thought they would not believe me. But I know what I saw, and I should've said something then, and maybe she wouldn't be here now." As Toby was finishing his sentence, he stared down the line of chained kids and locked eyes with this one girl who Adam couldn't help but think was the girl in Toby's story.

Meanwhile, back up on the hill, Anne was getting worried. It had been almost two hours since Andy left and horrible things were racing through her mind. "Do you think they have Andy?" asked Anne.

Jay hesitated for a moment then answered, "No, I don't think so. We would have heard him scream or something."

"But what if he couldn't?" asked Anne. "What if they covered his mouth?"

"No no," said Jay. "He would have bitten their hand."

"Well," said Anne, "what if they hit him across the head and knocked him unconscious? Or worse, what if they—"

"Don't say it," interrupted Jay. "Don't even think that way. Andy is a clever little dude, and at this point in time, we have to think positive."

"Okay," said Anne, "but if we don't hear something soon. I'm going to get my little brother."

Out of nowhere, they saw a speedboat approaching. A very nice size speedboat carrying boxes and crates. There was one guy onboard, navigating the vessel, but he was different from the other men. He didn't look like a pirate; he didn't dress like a pirate. He dressed like a businessman with slacks and a nice shirt, no tie, and he had shades on. This man drove the boat directly into the mouth of the cave as if he had been there before. The closer he got, Jay began to recognize him.

"It's Mayor Meyer," said Jay. "What is he doing here?"

This was very surprising because everyone thought Mayor Meyer was an upstanding guy, but clearly, he was up to no good. Obviously, the Mayor is in cahoots with the pirates. And with the Mayor's status, there was no chance that he's going to leave any loose ends. Jay knew he had to do something, and do it fast. So he and Anne went back into the woods. Jay knew he had to contact his Dad, but how? How could he notify his dad with no radio and no cellphone? So he decided to start a fire, knowing that the smoke from the fire, from this island would be an immediate indicator that something isn't right. Because everybody back on mainland are under the assumption that no one ever came to the island, this would warrant an immediate response, Jay thought.

But how could they start a fire? You see Jay was into girls and sports. He wasn't into the Boy Scouts and nature like Adam and Andy were, and he was unsure if he could start a fire on his own. If only they had thought of this before Andy left. "Hurry! We need something dry," said Jay. "Sticks or leaves, anything that's dry, so we can start a fire."

"But," said Anne, "because of the storm, everything is wet. The ground, the trees, and the leaves. Everything."

"I know," said Jay. "But we need something."

"What about this white stuff?" asked Anne. "Isn't it phosphorus?"

"Phosphorus?," repeated Jay.

"Yeah," said Anne. I remember reading about this island in school, and I read that, back when the climate was a lot drier, the island used to spontaneously burst into flames in little small spots on the island when the phosphorus had dried and reacted with the oxygen in the air. Since the island gets crushed with waves all the time, it stays moist, which prevents the fires from spreading. If we could collect enough of it and isolate it so that it could dry, then maybe we could start a fire."

"We'll need more than just phosphorus," said Jay. "A fire needs fuel, something to burn."

"What about our clothes?" asked Anne. "We could knock as much phosphorus off of our shirts as possible and use them to fuel the fire."

"Good idea," said Jay. "Take your shirt off."

"Excuse me," said Anne. "I don't think so. I have a dress on, not a shirt."

"But you said—" said Jay, as he was interrupted by Anne.

"I know what I said. And by we, I mean you. And by our, I meant yours."

Clearly defeated, Jay said, "Okay," as he ripped off his already torn shirt in true Hulkamaniac form. This caused Anne to be embarrassed but also intrigued as she slightly looked away with one eye closed and one observantly open. Trying to show no interest was a bigger fight than her taking on the pirates herself.

"I think this might work." said Jay as he brushed off his rag of a shirt. He could see small sparks from some of the already dried phosphorus reacting to the air.

Meanwhile, back in the cave, Mayor Meyer had gotten off the boat and was greeted by the Captain. "How is everything going?" asked the Mayor.

"Everything is going fine," said the Captain. "And with any luck, we'll be out of here by tomorrow night."

"To hell with luck," said the Mayor. "No matter what, come tomorrow night, this operation is over."

"What!" said the Captain. "This operation is over when I say it's over."

"I just want my little girl," said the Mayor.

"And you will get her," said the Captain. "Just do as you're told and keep your mouth shut, and you'll get her along with the rest of these little troglodytes."

"Now, did you bring the explosives?"

"Yes," said the Mayor as he was holding back tears.

"Good," said the Captain. "Unload your boat and go. Come back tomorrow night at nine to get your little girl and the others. But if anything goes wrong, they all will get it starting with your daughter. Now help him unpack the boat. Hurry. And, Mayor, leave the speedboat and take the malia back."

The malia is a wooden Hawaiian canoe. The Captain told the Mayor to take that canoe back partly to humiliate the Mayor but mainly because the Captain was going to use the speedboat to make his escape. You see, the Captain had no intentions of sticking around till the next night. In the Captain's mind, that night would be the last night of mining. As Andy overheard the Captain explain this to his men, Andy knew that the pirates would want to cover up their tracks. That meant that all the kids were now expendable, which also meant that something had to happen now. So just like the little pantry mouse, Andy snuck around, unnoticed, grabbing at things he would need to free Adam and the others. This was dangerous, but Andy wasn't going to sit around and do nothing.

Andy grabbed a stick of dynamite, some gunpowder, and the keys to unlock the prisoners' shackles. Andy stealthily made his way over to Adam and the others. Andy unshackled Adam and quickly gave him a hug because he was so happy that Adam was okay. One by one, the key was passed on until they had unlocked all twenty kids. A very heroic act on Andy's part, but how would they escape? You see, there was only one entrance to the cave, therefore, one exit, and there were four pirates and the Captain standing between them and the way outside. But it was now or never since, at that time, the Captain and the pirates were busy unloading the Mayor's boat and taking inventory.

CHAPTER 4

TOBY AND AALIYAH

As all the kids gathered around Andy, Toby asked, "Now what? How will we get out of here? There is only one way out, and the pirates have weapons."

"I know," said Andy, "but I have an idea. Follow me."

As Andy led them all deeper into the cave, he explained that, earlier, he had noticed water coming through the walls, and he could see tree roots. To Andy, that meant that the wall of the cave in that area could only be a few feet thick.

"Okay," said Toby. "But are we going to dig our way through with these small chisels? That would take days. The pirates will soon notice we're gone and come after us."

"I know," said Andy, "but no we are not going to chisel our way out. We're going to blast our way out."

"With what?" asked Adam. "How are we going to blast our way out?"

"With this," said Andy, holding a stick of dynamite with TNT marks clearly visible for all to see.

"Where did you get that?" asked Toby as the others oohed and aahed over Andy's surprise.

"I grabbed it from one of the boxes that Mayor Meyer just brought. I think he's working with the pirates."

"No no no," said Toby. "He is my girlfriend's dad. Andy, this is Aaliyah."

"Hi, Aaliyah," said Andy. "We thought you were dead. All the papers speculated that you were a victim of a serial killer, and later after it was reported that Toby was missing also, they thought that you two ran away together."

"No," said Aaliyah. "Toby just wanted to take me on a picnic, but my dad did not approve of me and Toby seeing each other. So Toby and I decided to have our picnic on this island so that we could have some privacy and not be bothered by others."

"So how was your picnic?" asked Adam.

"It was lovely," said Aaliyah. "Such a beautiful day. Being in this rainy climate, I must say that God's sun was truly in rare form as the breeze blew ever so softly, brushing past your face. It felt like the fur on the back of the chinchilla, I tell you! It was enough to leave a girl with permanent goosebumps, and to top it all off, my mom, who was visiting from New York, had cooked us fried chicken and buttermilk cornbread. And on that day, Toby was the consummate gentleman. Why he wouldn't even suggest a kiss. I had to be the one to make the first move."

"Yeah," said Toby. "As she was moving in toward me...well, that's when the pirates grabbed us. And I will never forget the words that came out of that wretched pirate's mouth: 'Sorry to break up your little romantic rendezvous,' and our only chance to kiss each other was stolen away from us by two godless pirates."

"But that was a year or so ago," said Adam. "You mean you guys haven't kissed since then?"

"No, we haven't," said Toby. "The pirates kept us apart on purpose to prevent us from escaping."

"But," asked Andy, "why is your dad helping the pirates?"

"Well," said Aaliyah. "After we were captured, the pirates discovered who I am and, therefore, who my father is and began to blackmail him, telling him that they would free me if he cooperated and brought them supplies that they needed."

"Yes," said Toby. "And that's why we should have stayed put."

"Come on, Toby," said Andy. "Do you really think the pirates or going to leave loose ends? No! They're going to get what they want and then they're going to blow this island sky high, and our remains will fall back to this godforsaken island like mere duck poo droppings. Is that what you want, Toby?"

"Well, no," said Toby.

"Good," said Andy as he walked toward the wall of the cave where the tree roots were protruding.

"Kiss her now!" yelled Adam.

"What!" said Toby. "No, not here, not now."

"Why not?" Adam said. "This is your chance to do it."

"Yeah, do it," urged the others standing around. They were as moved by Aaliyah and Toby's story as Adam was.

"All in favor," yelped Adam, "say aye."

As the others emphatically yelled their ayes out, Toby interrupted by saying, "This is not a democracy. This is not an election. There's no ballot in which you all can place a vote in this."

"Toby's right," said Aaliyah. "The mood is different now. It's just not the same."

"That might be true," said Adam, "but all I know is that on that beautiful day of the picnic when two young people were expressing their love for one another, those pirates stormed in and took something away from you, something that was so innocent and pure. So honest and true. And to add insult to injury, they separated you guys. And on top of all of that, they enslaved you and stole a year of your lives away that you can never get back. Look, I don't know if we will defeat these pirates and make it back to mainland. But what I do know is that we are at war, and you two have a chance to reclaim that kiss. That glorious kiss that the pirates so heartlessly gaffed from you would definitely deliver a mighty blow for the good guys. It might not win us the war, but it would definitely be remembered as our moral victory and the turning point in this battle. Now, how about that kiss for freedom, a kiss for all the little people, a smooch for the good guys—"

"Okay, Stonewall Jackson," said Toby.

As Toby sarcastically interrupted Adam's inspiring speech, Aaliyah launched toward Toby and planted a long-awaited but well-inspired kiss on Toby's dried, cracked lips. Not as romantic as first thought, but it did serve a purpose in picking up the spirits of the others.

As Aaliyah's kiss was being planted on to Toby's lips, several things were happening simultaneously. Anne and Jay had gathered enough dry phosphorus, and instantaneously, it began to burn as Anne, tore strips of Jay's dried shirt off to feed the flames. Mayor Meyer had gotten inside the malia and began to paddle off. The Captain had noticed that there were no drilling or chiseling noises coming from inside the cave, not even moaning sounds. So the Captain instructed the pirates to head back into the cave and insist that production be increased exponentially or else. The "or else" was more of an understood consequence rather than an expressed one from the Captain. So the pirates hurried back into the cave, but as they approached the worksite, to their surprise, the prisoners were nowhere in sight. As Aaliyah and Toby's faces separated, Andy lit the fuse of the dynamite. He rushed back toward the others for safety. The pirates reported back to the Captain, telling him of the prisoners escape. Knowing that the prisoners hadn't come out that way only meant that they were still somewhere in the cave. So the Captain ordered his minions to find them and dispose of them. As the pirates hurried off, the Captain began to pack his things, knowing that the prisoners escape was a signal that it was time to leave as well.

As the pirates were running down the cave, suddenly, there was an explosion. Andy's stick of dynamite had gone off, completely startling everyone on the island. Anne and Jay's fire had begun to send up plumes of smoke that could be seen for twenty miles in every direction.

Meanwhile, back on mainland, things have settled down a bit. So Sheriff Jacoby began to search for his boys. As the Sheriff drove down the street toward the beach, he was waved down by Mrs. Li, who is Anne and Andy's mom.

"Sheriff Jacoby," said Mrs. Li, "have you seen Anne and Andy?"

"No, I haven't," said Sheriff Jacoby. "I was just looking for my boys as well. I haven't seen them since this morning. But Adam did say that he was going of meet up with Andy later on here at the beach, so naturally, I decided to start my search here. When was the last time you saw your kids, Mrs. Li?"

"Well, Sheriff," said Mrs. Li, "I haven't seen Andy since this morning, and I was just with Anne earlier, preparing for her pageant, I say, about ten. She left to check on Andy, and I haven't seen or heard from them since. I tried Anne's cell phone, but for some reason, it seems to be off. Sheriff Jacoby, I'm worried I don't—"

"Look!" interrupted Sheriff Jacoby. "The smoke coming from the island. Mrs. Li, I think that smoke is the answer to some of our questions."

As Sheriff Jacoby hopped on the radio to dispatch search and rescue to the island, Andy and the others had finished climbing through the dynamite-induced hole in the wall of the cave. They began to grab branches, sticks, and rocks, anything they could see and move to fill the hole in the wall, knowing that the pirates would come up behind them. As the others followed, Andy led them back up the slippery hill where he had left Anne and Jay. Andy failed several times, and so did others. Andy proclaimed "It was a lot easier coming down than going up."

From an aerial view, the island shined against the beaming sun, which made it a perfect target for the ducks to bombard the island like a cartoon reenactment of Pearl Harbor, and yes, the ducks were the Japs. And sometimes because of the sudden hills that made up the island's terrain, ducks would just fly headfirst into the jagged landscape as if they were expendable Japanese kamikaze pilots crashing into the side of a USS battleship.

During the explosion, Mayor Meyer, who was in the malia heading back to mainland, quickly reversed his direction, knowing that there was no way the pirates had unpacked and prepped the dynamite for use that fast. Something was wrong.

Anne and Jay had heard the explosion as well, so they went to see what was happening. As they made it onto a clearing, they could see Andy and Adam plus a lot of other kids covered in dirt and mud, not to mention phosphorus powder and duck poo.

As Anne screamed out to Andy, they all heard an even louder scream that overpowered Anne's gleeful screech. It was Aaliyah being rustled and handled by two of the pirates, who had managed to squeeze through the hole. They begin heading back from the side of the island and toward the mouth of the cave. Toby, who had been helping the smaller kids make it up the slippery hill, yelled, "No!" and took off down the hill.

Andy said, "Wait, Toby!"

But either Toby didn't hear Andy due to the massive amount of adrenaline that must have been flowing through his body or Toby simply ignored Andy to rush off and save the love of his life. Now this is the stuff of novels. A heroic knight in shining armor, Toby (not so much!), gallops off to save his fair maiden Aaliyah, but in this novel, there was no way Toby was going to do this alone. As Anne and Jay made it down the hill, Adam and Andy were barking out instructions to the others. They sent half to the left side of the cave and the other half to the right side. Adam told Anne and Jay to go with him and Andy back through the dynamite hole, and all teams would meet at the mouth of the cave to rescue Aaliyah.

As Jay was going toward the hole, he looked off in the distance, and he could see movement across the horizon, and then he heard the faint sound of a chopper. "Look," said Jay. "It's my dad. He must've seen the smoke from our fire, Anne, and he's bringing in the cavalry."

Well, not exactly. Sheriff Jacoby was in a chopper with Mrs. Li, and his two deputies, Cal and Rory, who were in separate rescue boats. Those were really just fishing boats with a couple of life rafts onboard and a nice hand stenciled paint job on the side that simply read Rescue. Not necessarily a cavalry, but in total, they satisfied the makings of a poor man's armada.

As Jay and the others hurried through the hole and rushed toward the mouth of the cave just knowing that Sheriff Jacoby was on the way made them feel good and also served as one hell of a surprise that would surely catch the Captain and his pirates off guard.

As the pirates who had Aaliyah made it to the mouth of the cave, Mayor Meyer was there, and he could see the Captain and his men lowering boxes of emeralds onto his speedboat. The Mayor waited for his chance, and then he jumped into the speedboat and covered himself with a tarp. As the pirates entered the cave with Aaliyah, the Captain screamed "Where are the others? Is she the only one you caught?"

"Yes," said one of the pirates. "The others got away."

"Nonsense!" yelled the Captain. "What do you mean got away? This is an island, for god's sake. You should have made them swim to mainland to escape or sink them to the bottom of the sea. Surely, Davey Jones would want these peasants, but now they're sure to stage a coup to rescue this lovely pearl you two clams have brought back."

"All of a sudden, Toby sprints into the cave, demanding the pirates release Aaliyah. As the Captain began to laugh, he ordered his men to seize Toby. Two of the Captain's men came up from behind Toby to subdue him as Toby struggled with no success. It must've been at this point that Toby started to realize that it would have benefited him to have had a plan of action. Acting hastily usually worsens the problem and makes the outcome that much more of a horrible fate.

"What should we do with them, Captain?" asked one of the pirates.

As the Captain paused for a moment to think, he answered, "Put the girl in the speedboat and tie our hero to that crate of dynamite. Make him hug it, so he can experience a love like no other."

Since the others had escaped, the Captain knew that time was not on his side. The Captain ordered his man to put four crates of emeralds on the speedboat and to handcuff Aaliyah to the steering wheel. The Captain was going to use her as a bit of insurance in the process of him making his grand escape. You see, the Captain's plan was to take as many emeralds as the speedboat could hold and leave his own men to deal with the outcome. As the Captain made it to the boat, the enslaved teens rushed the cave's entrance, wielding sticks and stones that they had picked up along the way.

The Captain pushed one of his men out of the boat while yelling, "Go help the others," then the Captain immediately took off in the speedboat with Aaliyah on board. But what the Captain did not know was that they were not alone on board.

CHAPTER 5

ANDY

Back in the cave, Andy and the others had made it to the front of the cave and helped the other kids corner the pirates. With the pirates caught off guard, they had no weapons to fight with, so one of the pirates lit the fuse of the dynamite.

Jay yelled "Run, everybody. Run!"

So everyone took off toward the mouth of the cave in a stampede while Toby yelled, "Help!" Andy, being the only one who heard him or cared to hear him, came back to help. You see, Toby was handcuffed to the crate of dynamite in a bear hug embrace.

"Where is the key?" asked Andy.

"One of the pirates swallowed it," answered Toby. "You got to help me, Andy. The Captain has Aaliyah, and I have to help her." With no key and time running out, Andy had to think quick. As Andy was thinking, he wiped away some of the mud and sweat off just above his brow. And eureka, Andy stumbled upon a great idea to use the slippery mud that's mixed with duck poo as a lubricant to slide the chains up and off the crate, in effect, freeing Toby. But time was of the essence. So Andy worked hard and fast, scraping the mud off of his arms and legs and from the bottom of his shoes. Andy smeared the mud on to the chains as well as on Toby's arms and chest, accidentally getting a bit into Toby's mouth.

"Sorry, Toby," said Andy.

"That's okay," said Toby. "I think it's working. I can move. The mud is freeing me up." So Toby shimmied his way to the top, finally freeing himself from the intimacy in which he shared with the crate.

"Yes," said Andy, extremely excited that his plan worked. "Hurry, Toby. This way." Andy instructed Toby to run toward the back of the cave because Andy did not think they had time enough to make it to the opening of the cave before the dynamite went off. So they ran as hard and as fast as they could, trying to make it to the hole in the wall that Andy made earlier.

Meanwhile, back at the mouth of the cave, as the kids and the pirates pour out of the cave, to their surprise, there stood Sheriff Jacoby and his men along with Mrs. Li.

"Freeze!" yelled Sheriff Jacoby at the pirates as they stumbled out of the cave.

Excitedly Adam yelled "Daddy!" elated to see his dad standing there before him. It gave him a sense of safety and reassurance, knowing that his dad would handle the pirates and rescue them all off of the island.

As Anne embraced her mom, Mrs. Li said, "Thank God, you're safe" repeatedly. "Now where's your brother?" asked Mrs. Li as Anne clung on to her with gleeful tears pouring out of her eyes like water coming out of the business end of a hose. Anne gave no answer. "Anne!" said Mrs. Li, "where is Andy?"

"Andy!" yelled Anne. "He was with us in the cave, Mom."

One of the other kids spoke up and said, "Andy went back to help Toby. He was still handcuffed to the dynamite."

"Dynamite!?" said Mrs. Li.

"What dynamite?" asked Sheriff Jacoby as Adam started to explain that the pirates had lit the dynamite. Sheriff Jacoby instructed everyone to get as far away from the cave as possible. "Now! Hurry!" screamed Sheriff Jacoby.

As everyone had made it to the beach, the dynamite went off in the cave, and the explosion shook the entire island. Smoke poured out of the mouth of the cave as if a giant was smoking a stogie. Plumes of smoke raced skyward. It looked as if a volcano had erupted. Surely, the people back on mainland were at a loss as to what was happening on the island. A news crew that was in the area to cover the festivities had stuck around to report about the storm and all the damages it had caused. Bianca Berkowitz, channel 8 news reporter, was with this crew, and she was one of the first to notice the smoke coming from the island. "Well, guys" said Bianca, "looks like things have just gotten interesting. Call the station. We need a boat or a helicopter. Hell, I'll even take a submarine, but we need to get to that island ASAP!" Bianca Berkowitz a true news bloodhound. She could smell a good story from miles away. Literally!

Back on the beach, there was mayhem. The pirates were trying to escape as Sheriff Jacoby and his men did their best to corral these fiendish culprits. Adam, Anne, and Mrs. Li were all bawling their eyes out because they assumed the worst had happened to Andy. Mrs. Li and Anne had to restrain Adam, for he was trying with all his might to reenter the cave after Andy, screaming, "He would've come for me!"

All of a sudden, there was a loud bellow that came from the cave, causing all chaos to cease while everyone stared at the mouth of the cave. The cave began to implode upon itself. Wow! What an amazing sight, but sad because, in everyone's mind, this cave site has just become the burial place for Andy and Toby.

While silence still shrouded the beach, Adam began to speak, "He saved all of us. That he did." As Adam stumbled across the beach in a state of delirium, he continued to praise Andy's memory. "He was a hero to many and a saint to all!" exclaimed Adam as everyone looked at him and then back at the cave to view two figures emerging from its side, their silhouettes beaconing through the arid dust and particle debris caused by the collapse of the cave.

Several people said, "Look!" in breathy disbelief as Adam, unaware of the beholdings, rambled on in what must have been his idea of last words or some half-cocked eulogy for Andy. "Andy was the best friend a guy could ask for, you know? He was the kindest, most considerate person I've ever known, you know?"

As Adam continued to ask questions to which he expected no answers, he slightly turned to his right and looked over his shoulder to catch a glimpse of what he knew in his heart could not be so as silence fell on the beach and blanketed it like mustard gas.

Anne could not restrain herself from the overwhelming excitement that flooded her body with adrenaline, so much so that it brought her to unbearable exhaustion. And as she took a step toward the cave, she fell to her knees, so weighed down with emotions, both relief and fear, and weighed down from adrenaline overload, heat exhaustion, panic, and relief. Her speech impediment was brought on by confusion. As the shock of disbelief continued to hold the frozen onlookers in thrall, Anne offered up one word, one name that could thaw their glacial state. That word, my friends, that name Andy, its definition range from "hero," "survivor," "comeback kid," but most importantly—and this is pertaining to Adam—the name Andy meant one thing above all, "friend."

As Andy and Toby made their way down to the beach, the others broke out into applause. Anne finally mustered enough strength to make it over to her little brother and welcome him with open arms. Anne and Mrs. Li hugged and squeezed Andy so tight, it was as if he was a stuffed doll.

CHAPTER 6

BUSHIER BAY

Toby, extremely exhausted, excitedly made his way over to Sheriff Jacoby and mumbled inaudibly but very aggressively about something of urgency.

Sheriff Jacoby said, "Calm down. Calm down! What's the matter?"

As Toby was catching his breath, Cal, one of the Sheriff's deputies said. "Pint…Pint is that you?" The Pint Deputy Cal was referring to was Toby. You see, Toby was Cal's younger brother.

Cal said, "Toby!" as they both ran to each other, screaming out "oh my God." They embraced each other as only two loving siblings could, Cal in pure disbelief and Toby, happy to see his big brother. All of a sudden, Toby said "Aaliyah. Aaliyah! We have to go save Aaliyah."

Cal said, "Aaliyah's on this island?"

"No," said Toby. "The pirate's Captain has her on his boat. We have to go save her."

"But which way did he go?" asked Cal.

Sheriff Jacoby interrupted, "He must be going down the seaway, heading back to the ocean. Cal, hurry. Come with me to the boats. We'll head him off at Bushier Bay. Hopefully, before they hit the seaway."

"I'm coming too," said Toby.

"No, stay here and protect the others."

"No," said Toby. "I am the one who got Aaliyah in this predicament, and I'm going to do everything I can to get her out of it."

"Okay," said Sheriff Jacoby, "let's go." But before Sheriff Jacoby left, he called over Jay, Adam and Andy, and told them to keep everyone on the beach and that he would radio back to base and have them form a rescue crew to extract everyone off of the island and return them to mainland.

Assuming that the others on the beach would be safe until the rescue teams arrived, Sheriff Jacoby took Cal and Toby with him onto one of the rescue boats and instructed Rory, his other deputy, to board the chopper for aerial correspondence. Sheriff Jacoby wanted to be in the water in case of a physical confrontation with the pirate's Captain.

Meanwhile, back on mainland, Bianca Berkowitz had acquired a medium-sized speedboat for her and channel 8's crew to head over to the island. While heading to the island, the crew felt the rumbling caused by the dynamite explosion that collapsed the cave. Perhaps a delayed shockwave or maybe this happened simultaneously with the actual explosion. Either way, this made the crew that much more excited about what they would discover on the island. Due to the fact that channel 8's news crew was the only news station to get wind of these happenings made the story an absolute exclusive. Hello sweeps-week.

Due to Green Lake being such a small town, the local police often asked for volunteers and even had locals on call or standby in case of any type of emergency. So, naturally, many of the local residents from North Green Lake to South Shoreline have their very own personal police scanners and could eavesdrop on official police conversation at will.

With that being the case, when Sheriff Jacoby radioed back for rescue crews to rescue the kids on the island's beach who were thought to had ran away months back, well, you can imagine this sent Duck Country, whoops, sorry Badgers, this sent Mallard County into a frenzy. A swirling bowl of chaos, from the rootah to the tootah, ensued. Word spread like zombie germs from mailman to plumber, from Facebook to Twitter, from Duck to Badger. It didn't take long for channel 8 to get wind of the story and contact Bianca, who was already en route to the island.

Bianca, knowing that she needed to use this advantage that she had afforded herself, she began live broadcast en route to the island while she and the crew braved the waves and the marine environment that she so skillfully played up for the live cameras.

Meanwhile, the pirate Captain had finally made it to Bushier bay with Aaliyah. His intent was to board the ship. Okay, really it wasn't a ship, just a larger vessel. You would think it would have been this huge, dark, barnacle-infested pirate's ship but no. It was a thirty-four-foot Silverton Cabin motor yacht.

A yacht, people, that was in very good shape for a '95 series. Very clean, immaculate even had its own surround sound speakers and navigation, I mean all the state-of-the-art nautical equipment for your everyday avid sailors and/or pirate wannabes. It even had a love-seat for the steering wheel. Talk about a confident pirate. But these guys were not pirates. Just your everyday, run-of-the-mill white-collar crooks who prey on people who had less than them.

You see, these guys were from the big city, the Emerald City, Settlement, where all the big wigs and corporate suits ruined life for the locals by raising taxes, making parking impossible, and taking up road space so that this mad group of bikers can run wild in the city and endanger the lives of all.

Settlement, is no place I'd want to live. I tell you that, the big wigs have ran out the descendants of the people who work so hard to make Settlement, the booming metropolitan empire that it is today, or crumbling empire I should say. Since corporate enterprises and corrupt government leadership has taken over, Settlement, has not been the same. People use to look forward to going into Settlement, for shopping and enjoying the many fine eateries that the city had to offer. But not anymore, not poor people like us. Hell, you'd be lucky if they even let you in, and if they did, you probably couldn't even find parking. None that you could afford. In and out, it would be a waste of a thirty-minute ride both ways, and yet again Settlement, has banished you to the outskirts of metropolitan life. You are but mere onlookers to its towering majestic skyline. Back to Shoreline, back to Green Lake where you belong. Mallards can't fly with eagles, and these eagles are vultures trust.

Now back on mainland, near the shore, people, left and right, are jumping into boats, Sea-doos, canoes, anything that they could find that would float to get over to that island to see if one of the kids there was one of their sons, daughters, niece, nephew, cousins, or a kid that they used to babysit or teach. Everyone in town had some possible connection to one or more of these kids that had reportedly ran away, and now could potentially be on the beach of that island.

Back at Bushier bay, the pirate Captain started unloading emeralds off the speedboat, leaving Aaliyah handcuffed to the steering wheel. Now this was Mayor Meyer's big chance to let Aaliyah know that he was on board the speedboat and that everything was going to be all right. While Aaliyah was struggling at the steering wheel, trying to get free, she heard a noise coming from the back of the boat. A *pssst* sound at first. She thought it may have been a snake, so she curled up, and that's the moment, she spotted her dad in the fetal position under a black tarp with the Captain's sword resting on top of it. So surprised to see her dad on the boat, Aaliyah begin to cry. But when her eyes lock onto the Captain's sword, she became overwhelmed with fear. Not fear for herself, but fear for her father. Her mind became flooded with images of what the pirate Captain could do, and would do to her father. You see, although Aaliyah's dad was a very smart man, he was not very physical or athletic. So Aaliyah had no confidence in her father going up against the Captain and having any real success or being able to rescue her.

You see, the Captain stood all of 6'5" and weighed approximately three hundred pounds made up of pure muscles. As Mayor Meyer stood at only 5'8" and was bulbously shaped as well, he probably was not much of a match for the Captain.

As the Mayor attempted to stand up, Aaliyah began yelling, "No!" and causing her father to fall back to his knees.

"What are you yapping about?" asked the Captain as he made his way back to the speedboat.

Knowing she needed to say something so the Captain wouldn't become suspicious, Aaliyah replied, "Let me go you…" Okay, well, I can't type everything that Aaliyah called the Captain, but let me tell you, she had some choice words for him; words that made her father cringe under that black tarp with the Captain's sword on top.

As the Captain boarded the boat, he yelled at Aaliyah, saying, "Let's go, you foul-mouthed lil brat," or something to that affect. The Captain grabbed Aaliyah by the arm in an attempt to unlock the handcuffs, but Aaliyah fought back, kicking and screaming. With the Captain facing the front of the boat, his back was to the Mayor, so the Mayor knew that this was his chance to use the element of surprise to his advantage. So the Mayor stood up, grabbed the Captain's sword, and charged toward the front of the boat, half blinded from squinting and blinking to try and keep the sweat out of his eyes. His heart was beating fast. Faster than he had ever felt before, like pistons in a sports car moving one hundred miles an hour, the Mayor plunged the sword into a soft area between the Captain's buttocks and thigh. As this was happening, the Captain had managed to unlock the handcuffs when he felt the sheering cold blade enter his leg. Simultaneously, Aaliyah and the Captain screeched out in a perfect octave, a sound that can only be described as two sirens peacocking for one sailor's attention. Very quickly, the Captain spun around, grabbing the Mayor by the collar of his shirt as the Mayor grabbed the Captain's leg, causing him to experience excruciating pain from the wound caused by the katana sword that had skewered his leg in a shish kebab fashion.

As the two men were struggling, Aaliyah freed herself from the unlocked handcuffs. Now that she was free, she could help her father against the Colossus-sized Captain.

With all of her hundred pounds of body weight, Aaliyah jumped onto the Captain's back, causing him to lean forward. Aaliyah pushed the Captain overboard and into the shallow seawater. But the Captain did not let go of Mayor Meyer, his fist clenching tight on Mayor Meyer's collar like a vise grip. Both men splashed into the sea.

As Aaliyah reached out for her dad, she could hear the rotation of helicopter blades from a distance. "She looked up screaming daddy!" She could see the helicopter approaching.

In Aaliyah's mind, she knew it had to be a rescue crew. As Aaliyah's father and the Captain were tussling in the water, Aaliyah stood up, waving her arms at the chopper. All of a sudden, she could see a vessel coming down the seaway. It was Sheriff Jacoby and the others.

As the rescue boat moved further down the seaway the image of Aaliyah, and the two boats became clearer.

"Birdman to Nessy 1. Birdman to Nessy 1." It was Rory radioing the Sheriff from the helicopter.

"Go ahead, Birdman," said Sheriff Jacoby.

"I have a visual on said speedboat. One female on board, and it looks like two gents in the drink, having a belly-flopping contest," said Rory.

"Roger that. We're two clicks out. We will round up the contestants. Stick around and keep an eye on the prize."

"Received. Will do," replied Rory. And as Rory was saying over and out, the Sheriff yelled, "Full speed ahead," in a serious and urgent manner but with enough of a cliché-ish undertone that it warranted a bit of a smirk from Cal.

As the rescue boat got closer to the speedboat, Toby began to yell, "Aaliyah! Aaliyah!" And very quickly, the boat began to change directions. "What are you doing?" asked Toby.

"We are going to flank the speedboat and approach on the starboard side to prevent the Captain from trying to escape," said Sheriff Jacoby. But at that moment, this meant very little to Toby although he came from a long line of sailors and fisherman. The only thing on Toby's mind at that moment was getting to Aaliyah. So as Cal quickly turned the steering wheel, Toby dove into the water. His intention was to make a beeline for the speedboat where Aaliyah stood, waiting for him to come rescue her.

As romantic as this may sound, Toby hadn't swam in over a year, and we're talking October in the Northwest. The water was bone chillingly cold, so quickly, Toby's stroke was reduced to a dog paddle, but he was determined to make it to his love.

As Toby struggled in the water, he could hear Aaliyah's lovely voice yelling, "Hurry, Toby! You can do it! You're my hero." But what she really was yelling was "Boy, hurry up and get out of that water. You're going to freeze to death." As Toby was reaching the high levels of hypothermia, his body began to shut down. As his head slowly sank under the surface of the water, Toby could see the helicopter overhead. And as his mind began to shut down, to him it felt like he was a soldier in Vietnam, finally fulfilling his fate and about to get a chance to meet his maker. As the rotation of the helicopter blades slowed down, it almost mimicked Toby's faint heartbeat, he thought. He saw a blurry shadow, a watery silhouette approach, and then he saw black. Toby loss consciousness only seconds before he was pulled out of the water by Sheriff Jacoby and Cal, who had circled back around. The two rescued the love-struck fool from the clutches of the most notorious serial killer known to man, the sea. It has taken many lives even in the name of romance and heroism. These waters show no mercy and do not discriminate.

Meanwhile, as the Captain and the Mayor were wrestling in the shallows, the Captain could see the rescue boat approaching, and he also could hear the helicopter above. So the Captain knew he had to do something quick, so he rose up out of the water to deliver a mighty blow to Mayor Meyer, causing his body to plummet downward, smashing into the rocky bottom and bumping his head against the jagged rock, knocking him conscious. As the Captain rose out of the water, planting his feet on solid ground, he heard a bellowing voice coming from the heavens. Could it have been the voice of God, ready to chastise or even smite the Captain for his evil, wicked, and treacherous ways? No, it was just Rory in the helicopter, talking on the loudspeaker, commending the Captain to capitulate while yelling, "Freeze or I'll shoot."

But the Captain paid Rory little mind as he began to run toward the yacht. With the Captain not obeying Rory's commands, Rory began to fire rubber bullets at the Captain, striking him twice, once in the calf and once in his right shoulder. And although these were rubber bullets, believe me there was no bounce back. These bullets tore into the Captain's muscular flesh, causing the area to have ground zero–like impressions, leaving the area concaved and badly bruised, like meteorites violently crashing to the earth. This caused the Captain to fall to his knees in agonizing pain from the craters left in his body, thanks to Rory's sharp marksmanship.

At that time, Toby and the others had made it to the speedboat where Aaliyah stood, crying and yelling as she pointed toward her father, who was floating upside down in the water. In Cal's haste to reach the speedboat, he miscalculated his speed and distance, causing the rescue boat to crash into the speedboat and the rocky embankment, ripping holes in both vessels while throwing Aaliyah, Toby, and Sheriff Jacoby all overboard.

Toby swam around the two boats to reach Aaliyah while Sheriff Jacoby swam over to the Mayor. Struggling mightily, Sheriff Jacoby managed to pull Mayor Meyers lifeless body out of the water. Eerily as this was happening, it began to rain heavily as Sheriff Jacoby gave a last pull to get the Mayor's body out of the water, then he fell onto his back. Gazing up at the sky, Sheriff Jacoby could see the helicopter leaving, heading back to mainland, trying to outrun the massive storm clouds and heavy rain.

Sheriff Jacoby set up and began shaking and slapping the Mayor, who was unresponsive and morbid while checking for a pulse that was no longer there. The Sheriff's eyes became filled with tears as he glared out of focus through the heavy downpour. He could see Aaliyah and hear her sorrow-filled voice yelling, "Is he okay?" over and over again.

As the rain continued its torrential onslaught, everything became drenched and saturated. This caused the tides to increase rapidly and created an extremely dangerous situation for Sheriff Jacoby and the others. As Toby and Aaliyah made it over to Sheriff Jacoby, they began helping him drag the Mayor's corpse up the beach as the swelling tides crashed into them, knocking them off their feet repeatedly.

The trio did their best to drag the Mayor's 190 pound body out of the water and up the beach. But for some reason, deadweight seems to weigh a lot more, not to mention the condition they were in—heavy rains and lack of balance and strength. As the waves crashed down upon them, the sea proved to be too much as it battered the Sheriff and the two lovebirds something awful, causing the trio to loose their footing as well as their grip, unwillingly surrendering the Mayor's unanimated life vessel to the angry, unrelenting mob known as the tide. This game of tug-of-war was no contest at all as the Mayor's body swayed with the tide. It eventually took him under, leaving Aaliyah bawling her eyes out while being restrained by Toby.

As the sun peeked over the horizon, the sea had settled and the sky had cleared. Sheriff Jacoby, Toby, and Aaliyah all passed out on the beach from exhaustion, emotion, and fatigue. As Aaliyah awoke to her lament, she realized it had not been a bad dream. She had not awakened from a nightmare but woke up to continue that ongoing perversion. Her father was not only dead but was swallowed by the sea. Her eyes became faucets that drowned her will.

Cold, wet, and stranded, the point of life to Aaliyah became purposeless and minuscule, as Aaliyah began to walk into the sea with no intention of returning, Toby and the Sheriff began to awaken.

All of a sudden, Aaliyah stopped in the water waist deep. Toby asked the Sheriff, "What is she looking at?" As Aaliyah gazed across the horizon, she could see the hazy image of something approach, and whatever that something was, it was approaching extremely fast.

Not sure who could be manning that vessel, Toby and Sheriff Jacoby rushed into the water grabbing Aaliyah by the arms and gently escorting her out of the water. They took refuge behind the hillside. As they peered over the hillside to witness the approaching vessel, it became clear to them that it was more than one ship en route. There were many.

This truly frightened the Sheriff, for he knew that, with that many vessels, he and Toby would be outnumbered. Not including Aaliyah in their numbers for obvious reasons, the best thing to do would be to run, but their energy levels were depleted and their feet were in no condition to try and outrun anyone due to their prolonged immersion in those watery conditions. They all suffered from water aging and trench foot. That would prevent them from being agile enough to elude pursuers on foot. So this meant that they would have to take a stand and fight with all their might to protect Aaliyah. As Toby looked once again over the hillside, he said, "There are at least five boats approaching with at least three to five people aboard each boat. There is no way we can fight them all. Our best chance of surviving is to hide."

"How do you propose we do that?" asked the Sheriff.

"Well, we are on a beach," said Toby. "Let's use the sand to bury ourselves alongside the hillside and pray they don't find us."

With no bright idea of his own, Sheriff Jacoby began taking orders from Toby, who was a visionary on this one. It took them almost an hour to cover Aaliyah and themselves completely in sand alongside the hillside.

CHAPTER 7

MOTLEY RESCUE CREW

Little did they know, the approaching boats carried no pirates, and no one that wanted to hunt them or bring harm to them. It was just a rescue crew led by Andy, Adam, Jay, Anne, and Mrs. Li. Accompanying them was Deputy Rory, who felt that he could be more help to the Sheriff on the ground than in the air. And with him was an eclectic mix of the town's folks who wanted to do anything they could to help. Let's see, there was Coach Daniel Gillespie, he is the coach of the reigning champion Green Lake Ducks; also Uncle Ken and his grandkids; Sidney, the bike guy who owned the local bicycle repair shop in town; and Farmer Sam, who was reunited with his oldest son who was held prisoner in that cave by the pirates for over a year. And bringing up the rear echelon of this group was Bianca Berkowitz and her channel 8 news crew. And last but not least, there was Beethoven, the town's local troubadour, who performed on the sidewalks of both Green Lake and Shoreline. Bianca had interviewed everyone on the beach and documented their stories. Her crew had shot footage of the captured pirates and collapsed cave with many of the shots in need of editing due to multiple slipups by the cameramen. I mean literally. They were slipping on the duck poo that covered that island like red plastic covering a store-bought babybel.

Only thing left for Bianca was to interview the Sheriff or so she thought, unaware of the Mayor's demise or the evolving romance between Aaliyah and Toby.

And while the demise of the Mayor was bad news to most, for an A1 bloodhound like Ms. Berkowitz, this was a gravy train that she would most willingly eat up.

As this Motley rescue crew made it to the banks of the seaway, they ran into floating debris peppering the shallows like remnants of an explosion. While everyone paused and stared into the water, Andy began barking out orders like a general under siege. "Listen up, everybody" said Andy "when we reach the beach we're going to break up into search parties. Everyone in my boat will come with me, and everyone in Deputy Rory's boat will go with him, and so on. And remember to assign someone to stay with the boats. We are the search party. We don't need anyone searching for us."

While Andy continued to delegate, no one was recalcitrant or argumentative. They knew he knew what he was doing, or did he? The last order he yelled out was "Stay alert. Stay alive," something he had heard once on *Saving Private Ryan*. Andy was a born leader like his father. People would just line up to be led by him. Andy's only fear was not to try at all.

So as they reached the beach, they all began to follow Andy's orders to the letter. Andy and his crew took the middle of the beach while the other crews went along the sides. With Deputy Rory's crew going left along the water, and Uncle Ken's crew with Bianca and the cameramen going right along the hillside. It wasn't long before Uncle Ken began to see footprints in the sand. As Uncle Ken was bringing it to the attention of his crew, Jayce, Uncle Ken's grandson whispered, "Listen....you guys hear that? It's coming from over there."

Altogether everyone turned their attentions toward the right side of the hillside in a dark area that didn't receive the sun's light.

As Jayce lead the others closer to the sun's blind spot, that sound got louder and more distinct. It sounds as if someone was weeping uncontrollably, and Jayce knew where it was coming from. As

Jayce took off, Uncle Ken yelled, "Wait!" But Jayce was determined to reach the location of that sound. "Can anyone see him?" asked Uncle Ken.

With Uncle Ken receiving a flurry of no's and silence from his crew, he began fashioning a torch, using a stick he found on the beach and one of Jayce's old shirts he had brought with him. While Uncle Ken was making his torch, the others stood around, tapping their flashlights, wondering what Uncle Ken was thinking.

The camera crew with the camera light shining as well received a whisper from Bianca saying, "Keep rolling" as she stepped in front of the cameras that were trained on Uncle Ken. And what seemed like a bout with madness, Bianca began reporting, "As insanity set in on this epic quest to find missing loved ones…"

All of a sudden, there was an echoing voice that yelled out. "Over here!"

As Uncle Ken successfully lit his torch, he yelled back, "Jayce!"

Uncle Ken rushed into the darkness, followed by the others. Uncle Ken's torch and the others' flashlights illuminated the darkness. About two minutes in to the darkness, they spotted Jayce, standing next to the hillside with his hands up, signaling for them to be quiet. Noisily, the camera crew had caught up to the others where the weeping ceased as the hillside began to move. "Over here, Jayce" said Uncle Ken.

But before Jayce could move, he was grabbed by something or someone who was covered in muddy hillside clay. As Amana, Jayce's little sister and Uncle Ken's granddaughter, screamed out in fear, Uncle Ken began to plead with the muddy monstrosity to please just let Jayce go, calling him "the boy."

During this standoff, Andy's crew and Deputy Rory's crew were both alerted by the yelling and commotion from the hillside and had made it over to Uncle Ken's crew and were surprised by this standoff between Uncle Ken's crew and this unknown individual. All of a sudden, out of the hillside emerged a second figure. A smaller figure covered from head to toe in sand and clay. As Amana was filling Andy and the others in on what was happening, Andy looked up as the second figure emerged from the hillside. "Aaliyah!' said Andy. "Is that you?"

"Andy," said the first figure, who, by this time, Andy and Adam both assumed was Toby.

"You know them?" asked Uncle Ken.

"Yes," said Andy. "I rescued them once from the, caves and now I get the privilege of doing it again. This time properly."

As Aaliyah and Toby realized that they were being rescued, they both fell to their knees in relief. Adam and Andy rushed over and hugged them as Amana brought over water for Aaliyah to drink, knowing that she must be extremely parched.

As everyone rejoiced in having found Toby and Aaliyah, Deputy Rory look perplexed as he raised his hand in the air to get everyone's attention and quiet them down. And then he asked, "Where's the Sheriff...and the Mayor?"

When the deputy asked this, Aaliyah began to cry. She went from being relieved to sobbing uncontrollably. Then Toby hugged Aaliyah's shoulders in an attempt to console her. He told Deputy Rory that the Sheriff was still in the hillside.

Quickly, Deputy Rory rushed to the hillside, pulling the unconscious Sheriff out of a hole and onto the beach where Deputy Rory began performing CPR on Sheriff Jacoby. Everyone seemed very worried for the Sheriff. Deputy Rory asked everyone to please back up and give him some room.

Looking up at Toby while he hugged Aaliyah as Aaliyah continued to cry, Amana asked, "Why is she still crying like that? The Sheriff is going to be all right."

"It's not the Sheriff, it's the Mayor!" said Toby.

Overhearing Toby's response to Amana's inquiry, Bianca, with cameras "still rolling," asked, "What's that about the Mayor?"

Just as Toby was about to enlighten everyone about the Mayor's demise, the Sheriff began to cough as he was struggling to breathe and regain consciousness. Deputy Rory had revived the Sheriff, who was struggling to get something out.

"What is it, Sheriff?" asked Rory. As everyone listened, the Sheriff became panicked, asking over and over, "Where is he? Where is he?"

"Who is he talking about?" asked Uncle Ken. "The Captain?"

"No! Not the Captain," answered Deputy Rory, trying his best to make out what the Sheriff was mumbling.

This caused Bianca to turn to Toby, asking him, "Where is the Mayor?"

"He's dead," said Toby. "The Mayor is dead, and the sea claimed his body."

As everyone stood there frozen in shock by Toby's announcement, the Sheriff yelled out, "Cal? Where is Cal? Has anyone seen him?" asked the Sheriff.

"The last time I saw Deputy Cal was on the rescue boat, just before the storm," said Aaliyah.

"He must have gone after the Captain alone," said Deputy Rory.

"That's it. We must form a search party," said the Sheriff.

"Calm down," said Uncle Ken. "The sun is going down. It's almost dark. We need to set up camp, start a fire, and rest up for the night."

"No," said the Sheriff. "We need to go find him. His life could be in danger."

"We get that!" said Uncle Ken, "But it's late, and we have children with us. Let's rest up till sun up, and I promise we can roll out first thing in the morning."

These words from Uncle Ken seemed to calm the Sheriff down. As everyone pitched in to help set up camp before dark, Bianca Berkowitz continued to interview Toby and Aaliyah on the circumstances behind the Mayor's death. With Bianca saying, "Okay, cut. That's enough for tonight." Those words from Bianca were the last words spoke on the beach that night.

"Good morning, sleepyheads," said Uncle Ken as he awakened everyone to the smells of bacon, sausage, and eggs that he cooked with the rendered bacon fat, leaving the air heavily saturated. The smells permeated throughout the beach, hugging the morning dew like candy coat on a skittle. It was approximately 6:30 a.m., a little later than Uncle Ken and the Sheriff had wanted to get up. And speaking of the Sheriff, he woke up cranky from a headache that wouldn't wait a minute. The sun hadn't quite illuminated the beach fully. There were still blind spots on the beach that kept it pretty dark for that time of day.

Everyone gathered their things and prepared themselves to continue the search for Cal and possibly the pirate's Captain, who most suspected was far gone from that area by then.

During the night, Anne had shared a tent with Jay. That's right, Jay, her grade-school crush. The guy she had grown to loathe for his testosterone, adrenaline-overloaded bravado. Somehow, they had rekindled their flame since Duck Poo Island—a name coined by Andy when interviewed by Bianca and willingly adopted by the others. So as Anne, for just a moment, tore herself away from Jay to brush her teeth, she gave herself a chance to think about Andy and then Adam and then the fact that, amongst everyone packing, she did not see either one of them.

As Anne began to ask the others if they had seen her brother and Adam, she did her best to stay calm to not invoke panic. But word got back to Mrs. Li, and she began to yell out to Andy.

"What's the deal with all that noise?" asked the Sheriff.

"It is Mrs. Li," said Deputy Rory. "Apparently her son has gone missing."

"Well, I can assure you, if Andy has gone missing, Adam's right there with him," said the Sheriff.

As everyone was searching about, looking for signs of the loss duo, Sheriff Jacoby pulled his binoculars out and began to scan the perimeter. He climbed up the hillside to get a better vantage point.

"Do you see them?" asked Mrs. Li, but the Sheriff was quiet and distracted. You see, he did see something, something gruesome and horrible. It was a wreckage about the size of a yacht, give or take. And he did see the boys, and he could tell that they were okay, just investigating the wreckage.

"All right. Everyone, listen up" said Sheriff Jacoby. "I am going to need everyone to follow me and stay close together. No one strays."

While Sheriff Jacoby was handing out orders like demands, Mrs. Li walked up to him and just stared at the Sheriff as if she were waiting for something. Maybe she was waiting for a break in his sentence to tell him something or maybe she was waiting for him to give her specific instructions. Or maybe she was just waiting for him to pay her some attention, so she could slap him for seeing something through his binoculars and not telling her what he had seen. An explanation on that would have been nice, but the Sheriff knew exactly what she wanted. She wanted to be included in the search, and she knew just as he knew. He was going to need her to stay back by the boats with Aaliyah, Anne, and some of the younger kids. But instead of telling Mrs. Li this, he just walked off and instructed Jay and Toby to round up, basically the women and kids to stay back with the boats. This angered Mrs. Li something awful, for every step Sheriff Jacoby took away from Mrs. Li, her eyes began to swell with liquid and as her eyes reached their maximum limit a heavy but singular tear rolled down her right cheek as to hide this act from the Sheriff who's commencement was to her left. As Mrs. Li took a step to her right, stood Bianca and her camera crew " still rolling." Bianca, having seen the whole dramatic scene play out, walked up to Mrs. Li and offered to stay back with the kids. The cameramen stared at each other in disbelief, for this was a side of Bianca no one had seen before.

Was it possible that this career-driven, hard-nose bloodhound has a heart? This caused the left eye of Mrs. Li to fill with liquid and to overflow, offering up a single tear that rolled down her cheek and reached her chin. Just at that moment, Sheriff Jacoby looked back. This was a tender moment for the ages. But it was interrupted by Mrs. Li's response to Bianca's offer. Not being one to be pitied, Mrs. Li replied, "Bianca, can you cook?" As Bianca, surprised by the question stood there silently, "I didn't think so," said Mrs. Li. "There's no story here. The story's out there. You go find my boy, and you'll find your story, Bianca." And after that, Mrs. Li just stormed off toward the boats, leaving Bianca standing there in awe of Mrs. Li's strength and humility but also embarrassed by her own attempt to open herself up for another. Bianca just stood there, exposed, paralyzed by her own vulnerability. For the first time in her life, she owned that moment.

CHAPTER 8

RECLAIMED JEWELS

It took Sheriff Jacoby and his posse about forty-five minutes to reach the opposite end of the hillside where he had spotted the boys and the wreckage. As the posse approached, they found two exhausted little boys covered in muddy clay from head to toe. They had found the Captain's yacht. It had been bashed against the hillside repeatedly and torn into a million pieces. The boys were exhausted from picking up the emeralds in which the Captain had loaded onto the yacht. They were scattered in the shallow waters and along the beach.

"What were you boys thinking?" asked Sheriff Jacoby, but neither Adam nor Andy answered the Sheriff. They were so tired and drowsy that they just fell back onto their individual bag of gems and gazed up at the Sheriff, who stood directly in front of them, blocking out the sun. As his silhouette moved slowly, the sun's rays peeked out from behind his head, creating an angelic halo effect. Adam and Andy dropped to their knees with one arm around their individual bag of gems. Their free arm sent up Hail Mary air crosses like no tomorrow.

As Sheriff Jacoby got closer, the boys began to paw at him, and as they squinted, the Sheriff finally came into full focus. This calmed the boys down, and they became quite. As Adam and Andy looked at each other, they broke out into uncontrollable laughter, causing the Sheriff, Uncle Ken, and the other to join in on the laughter.

That's when Sidney, the bike guy said, "What were y'all doing, protecting your jewels from God."

This caused everyone to laugh harder. And then Farmer Sam chimed in, "What were y'all going to do! Claw God's eyes out?" His comment caused everyone to laugh even harder. It quickly became clear to Adam and Andy that the others were no longer laughing with them but at them.

"You boys know you can't keep them, right?" asked Deputy Rory, still laughing.

"What are you talking about?," said Andy. "These jewels are ours. We found them fair and square."

"Look around, boys," said Sheriff Jacoby. "You're sitting smack dab in the middle of a crime scene, and every jewel in those bags is evidence."

"Evidence!" said Andy, "Crime scene! This here ain't no crime scene. This was an accident at sea. Hell, if we would not have come over here to rescue you, we would not even have seen all of this debris. This debris would have eventually got caught in a gulf steam and ended up a hundred miles that a way." Andy pointed in the direction of the ocean. "And these jewels, days later, even weeks later, would have still been right here in the shallows amongst these worthless rocks and pebbles."

"Boys, look," said Sheriff Jacoby. "Be sensible. Those emeralds come from off that island where the pirates used slave labor, child labor even, to harvest them. Them being here on this beach now, well, that was just the pirate Captain tampering with evidence. It's still evidence, boys. You can't keep it."

"But," said Adam.

"No buts," said Sheriff Jacoby as Adam and Andy brokenheartedly stared out at everyone, seeing every individual standing still in their own personal space. Andy locked eyes with Bianca and her camera crew " still rolling."

"Miss News Lady, come here," said Andy as Bianca instructed her cameramen to follow her. She braved the shallows, which surely destroyed her candy-apple stilettos in the process. But shoes can be bought again but, stories are born, birthed from situations and circumstances, be it tragedy or triumph. I am sure that that little blurb went through Bianca's head as she approached the boys.

"Miss News Lady," said Andy. "Look, you can help us out, right?"

"I'm not sure," said Bianca.

Andy pleaded with Bianca, asking her to please document what they had found and the fact that they were alone on the beach when she arrived with the others. As Bianca looked at the boys and then at the Sheriff, she said, "Okay, I am sure that there is some statute of law that will protect your findings."

"Like what?" asked Andy.

"Well," said Bianca, some type of lost and found clause that could get you boys your property back. But it wouldn't be until after the investigation." Bianca, doing her best to appease the boys and help the Sheriff out too, she finally was able to make peace and convince the boys that they had a shot at keeping their jewels.

As Bianca received an okay from Adam and Andy, Sheriff Jacoby and Deputy Rory helped Adam and Andy to their feet and gave them both a canteen filled with water and a link of sausage from that morning's breakfast feast prepared by Uncle Ken.

As Adam and Andy continued to rehydrate along the beach's edge, the Sheriff and the others wandered up the beach, looking for whatever they could find to explain to them what had happened to the yacht, to the Captain, and possibly to Cal. No one was sure what had happened to him. While everyone roved the beach, looking for clues, Adam and Andy were resting on the beach, talking about what they were going to buy with the money they were going to get from their reclaimed jewels.

"Well, let's see," said Andy. "First off, I'm going to buy myself a Range Rover!"

"A Range Rover?" questioned Adam.

"Yes!" answered Andy. "It's a status car!"

"A status car?" questioned Adam.

"Yes!" answered Andy. "This type of vehicle says something, you know. It makes a statement."

"What statement?" asked Adam.

As Andy threw both arms out to his sides like Michael Jackson did in his "I'm Bad" video, Andy said, "It says, 'I have arrived.'"

"Arrived where?" asked Adam.

"You know," said Andy. "You made it to that destination and such."

"Oh!" said Adam. "My brother Jay, he got this old Honda Civic from my pop, who had it way back when he was in college, and it is still arriving today as long as Jay remembers to change the oil and check the tires."

"Whatever," said Andy. "You don't get it."

"Of course, I don't get it," said Adam, "because it's stupid. You don't even have a driver's license."

"I know that," said Andy. "I'm going to park it in the driveway until I get my learner's permit."

"Okay," said Adam, "that's a plan, but there is one problem."

"What's that?" asked Andy. "You currently don't have a driveway."

"Oh yeah!' said Andy. "You're right. Well, maybe that's the second thing on my list to do. And the first is to buy my mom a very nice house with a four-car garage, so I can park the Range Rover when I get it."

"Well, that's cool," said Adam, "but I want to do something memorable, something that will leave a legacy for years to come."

"But we're twelve!" exclaimed Andy. "We need to have fun."

"And we will," said Adam. "I think we need to buy the island and rename it Duck Poo Island."

Andy stood there, frozen and in shock from some of the most beautiful words he had ever heard uttered from another human being. He told Adam to go on, basically telling Adam to elaborate on that idea and to tell him more. As a colossal smile appeared on Adam's face, he continued to explain his idea to Andy. "We could make it a go-kart attraction and build tracks all the way around and through the entire island and rebuild and secure the cave and make it the focal point of the island."

"Yeah," said Andy. "But what about the duck poo? It would make the tracks very slippery causing the carts to slip and slide all over the place."

Not taking a second to reply, wanting to keep Andy in the moment, Adam said, "No two rides would ever be the same, and on the go-carts, we could put pro traction tires on for grip, and we could install an automatic sanding system to improve traction."

"I like that," said Andy.

"Cool!" said Adam. "We could also put up gutter rails or guard-rails to prevent anyone from veering off course. What do you think?"

But as Andy was about to respond, there was an outcry, "Over here." As the boys looked up, they saw everyone running toward the hillside. So they helped each other up and made their way over to the others where they saw the Sheriff and Deputy Rory moving some-thing. And as they got closer, it became clear to them that it was the pirate Captain's dead body. They also could see Uncle Ken and some of the others crowded around another body. It was Deputy Cal's body. Later, they saw that Deputy Cal was alive but not so much kicking. He had sustained a broken leg and several bruised ribs, but he was alive.

The Sheriff, Deputy Rory, and Uncle Ken held a conference at the far end of the beach to discuss how they were going to get Cal back to the boats and what they were going to do with the Captain's body. Everyone else crowded around Cal, giving him the shirts off of their backs to keep him warm and force feeding him Earl Grey tea and tiny strips of beef jerky to help increase his core temperature.

As Adam and Andy stood there, looking at the others caring for Cal and worried about how they were going to transport him back to the boats, Adam and Andy felt a bit ashamed for sitting on the beach for so, long talking about what they were going to buy themselves while the others were searching for Cal. Well, it just made them sick to their stomachs. Andy, possibly feeling the worst, just walked off to the water's edge and stared off into the horizon. As Adam walked over to comfort Andy, he could see that Andy was really upset, but Adam did not know the words to say. So he just stood there, mute with one arm on Andy's shoulder, just to let Andy know that he was there for him. All of a sudden, Andy swung around, looking Adam dead in the eye and Said, "I am done with this hero crap."

"What do you mean?" asked Adam. "I am an adventurer, a risk taker, an explorer, a swashbuckling romantic. Hell, we're more like the pirates than we are like the cops."

"Yeah!" said Adam.

"Minus the slave labor and apparent lack of hygiene," " I hate cops," said Andy.

"No!" said Adam, "don't say that."

"I know," said Andy, "but I'm just done. I mean this hero crap is for the birds, you know? I mean the cops are the real hero. They signed up for this crap, I didn't. I'm no hero. I am just a voyager, a venturer, but I don't want to be the pirate. I want to be the one that brings the pirate down and claim his treasures for my own. And I can't do that, running elbow to elbow with the law."

"Listen," said Adam. "I know you're having a moment of crisis, but don't ever say you're not a hero. It's what you do. You have more courage in your pinky than most people have in their entire bodies. You are CBK, the Come Back Kid! You love the advantage."

"I love the booty," said Andy.

"You want the excitement," said Adam.

"I want my jewels," said Andy.

"You know," said Adam, "you're not as selfish as you think you are. I have seen countless selfless acts in which you have performed for others. Like when my mom locked herself out of the house and you climbed up to the second floor window that was open. You went in and unlocked the front door. That was so cool."

"Yeah!" said Andy. "But anybody could do that."

"You're right, but you were five, and I know, at five, that wasn't something that I could do, and you did it with such grace. You made it look effortless. That's the moment I knew you were destined for greatness. Come on, Andy. If we ever needed you to come back, it's now." As Adam was giving Andy his best, most heartfelt inspirational pep talk ever, Sheriff Jacoby came over and interrupted Adam by asking them both, "What do you think is the best way to transport Deputy Cal back to the boats?"

Sheriff Jacoby had seen over the years the things Adam and Andy where capable of doing. The Sheriff had great respect for their abilities to get things done, even if he didn't always agree with their methods. "Well," said Andy, "I guess we could take a large piece of debris from the obliterated yacht and tie Cal to it and use the string to guide the debris in the water. And that way, we could walk along the edge of the water to return to camp."

"Yeah!" said Adam co-signing with Andy. "It would be a lot easier than carrying him the whole way and faster too."

"Thanks, guys," said Sheriff Jacoby. "That sounds like a solid plan. I knew I could count on you, boys."

This brought a huge smile to Andy's face. Just seeing how pleased the Sheriff was with his idea really helped to pick his spirit up. "Okay, listen up, everyone," said Sheriff Jacoby. "Gather your things. We have a plan on transporting Cal back to camp, but we only have about three hours until sunset, so let's get move."

With the Sheriff's speech and the apparent time constraints, it became obvious to all that they would have to spend at least one more night on the beach back at camp. But their mission was successful, so it would be a lot more fun tonight than it had been, just knowing that when they wake up, they were heading home. That made everyone want to enjoy the moment to the fullest.

"But what about the Captain's body?" asked Deputy Rory.

"Well," said the Sheriff. "He's too heavy for us to transport back to camp. I think we are going to have to leave his body here for the investigators to deal with."

"You mean whatever is left of him," said Coach Gillespie.

"What are you yapping about, Danny?" asked the Sheriff, who really didn't like the coach at all. This was one of those Duck, Badger alumni issues that go way back to when they were in high school, with the Sheriff being a Badger and the coach being a Duck. There's bad blood there, and it existed in everything they did.

"Well," said the coach, "I'm just saying, by the time CSI gets here, the seagulls and vultures will have picked all the meat off the Captain's massive size bones, is all."

"Okay then," said the Sheriff, "how about you stay back and tend to this criminal while the rest of us get this hero back to his family and loved ones?"

That was an intense moment. As the Sheriff turned to leave, he threw his arm up in the air to signal to the others that it was time to go. But the coach chose not to stay back despite his protests for the Captain.

As Sheriff Jacoby and his crew made it back toward the beach and saw Mrs. Li and the others, both sides began to rejoice as Andy pulled out his spyglass, which he had found on the beach along with the gems that were confiscated from him and Adam, all 110 pounds of them. By the way, they were being transported back to camp by Deputy Rory, who was so animated about the boys not keeping them. Talk about giving the opposition a workout.

Through Andy's spyglass, he could see the warm smiling faces of his mom and his sister. This made Andy take off running with Adam right behind him. As they ran ahead of the others to the beach to embrace their friends and loved ones, the reunion turned into a full-blown party. The troubadour broke out banjos and harmonicas, the others started a barn fire by burning pieces of the debris, clothing, and trash while they danced around that blazing inferno for hours. Uncle Ken cooked all the food that he had brought for that trip—Yukon gold potato, beef stew, and Uncle Ken's signature dish, Peking duck, which he had prepared at his restaurant. Uncle Ken also made hot tea with a bit of rum in it to help keep everyone warm and in good spirits. Bianca, whose camera crew was "still rolling," also joined in on some of the celebrating. They all had a great time for hours, and then they begin to pass out one by one, until the beach became silent and the flames died down. The fire had gotten so big that now with no flames being visible, the embers were still capable of warming the entire beach.

CHAPTER 9

MAINLAND

As the morning sun shined over the hillside and spilled into the sea, sounds of seagulls disturbed the slumbering ravers. The seagulls scrounged for discarded scraps of food that littered the beach. Slowly, everyone rose up to their feet like Walking Dead extras as the Sheriff instructed them to line up shoulder to shoulder and walked the entire beach, picking up all the trash and unnatural materials that they had brought to the beach. This was very green of him, not wanting to disturb the natural ecosystem more than they had already done.

Finally, everyone loaded into their boats and began to head back up the seaway toward home. It was bitter sweet for them. You see, they all had had such a great time on the beach that they were a bit sad about it now that they were heading home. The trip back to mainland would be approximately an hour and thirty minutes. But for those with a heavy heart like Aaliyah, it would probably seem longer, or maybe not long enough. For the end of that trip signified the beginning of accepting the reality of it all.

Docking back at mainland was the end of an adventure and the start of bereavement, mourning, wakes, paperwork, interviews, interrogations, and on and on. It seemed never ending. The bliss of the adventure made you want to stay at sea, and the chaos of reality made you want to drown at sea. Everyone was in deep thought; the boats were quite. Only sporadic navigation orders from the Sheriff could be heard along with the inaudible chatter from the radio, which meant that they were picking up a signal. All of a sudden, helicopters and boats could be seen and heard as they approached Duck Poo Island. They could see swarms of people collecting materials from the beach and inside the collapsed cave.

"Who are they?" asked Andy, "What are they doing?"

"This, my boy," said Deputy Rory, "is what we like to call the circus."

"The circus?", repeated Andy."

"Yes," said Deputy Rory. "Let's see. We have the FBI clowns and the forensic freak show, a bunch of monkeys in suits. If you asked me, I mean what an attraction, right?

"Oh boy!" said Amana. "Can we go?"

"No," said the Sheriff. "We would just get in the way, and they have their hands full, plus we all need to get home and get cleaned up. You guys smell like seashells."

This made everyone laugh as they all cruised past Duck Poo Island on their way back to mainland.

It had been about thirty minutes since they passed Duck Poo Island and heading back to mainland, when, to their surprise, the beachfront was covered with the townsfolk. There were EMTs, fire trucks from two towns, Ma Jones and Pa Jones from the Mom and Pop shop. The teachers from the schools, construction workers, and all the kids that were rescued from Duck Poo Island and their parents were waiting there to greet the Sheriff and his brave crew. But little did the Sheriff and his crew know that Bianca and her camera crew "still rolling"—in the rear boat had regained their signals and had been broadcasting live for the last forty-five minutes. That's what gave everyone on mainland the heads up that the crew was approaching. The beachfront looked like homecoming, almost exactly like the moment Adam, Andy, Anne, and Jay decided to go pedal boating.

As the boats docked, the swarming crowd began to cheer as the EMTs rushed down to take charge of the injured. With Deputy Cal being the only injured person in the party, the paramedics gave him their full attention. And for the others, they received bottles of water and orange slices that were provided by both Line High's and Lake High's booster clubs. The atmosphere was thick with celebration and glee as the pyrotechnic guys introduced their presence with a barrage of heavy-duty fireworks overhead. And right when Adam and Andy exited their boat, the crowd grabbed them and hoisted them overhead. This was due to Bianca's live reporting. She had revealed in her report that Adam and Andy where the true heroes in this saga. The boys ate it up, Adam especially. You see, Adam had never been included in one of Andy's heroic exploits before, so this was a real treat for him.

It was exciting. Everyone cheered for these heroes as they made their way from the docks to Front Street. The EMTs took Deputy Cal to the hospital. He was in need of some emergency surgery. But right before they left, Cal seemed a bit happy. He seemed more grateful than anything else. I'm sure, lying out on that beach in that cold, wet environment must have played tricks on his mind, not knowing if anyone would come for him, not knowing if he could hold on. That must have been the saddest and loneliest period in Cal's young life.

Everything was peaceful and happy as they all watched the ambulance ride off with Cal to the hospital with Aaliyah and Toby following in South County's ambulance. As everyone gathered on Front Street, out of nowhere, four all-black Suburbans pulled up. There were two guys dressed in black in the lead vehicle and only drivers in the other three. The two got out and approached the crowd, saying, "I am Agent Williams. I need you all to come with me, please."

"For what?" asked the Sheriff.

"Who are you?" asked Uncle Ken.

At that moment, Agent Williams flashed his FBI badge and said, "I need Sheriff Jacoby, Deputy Rory, Aaliyah Meyer, Toby Taylor, and Calvin Taylor to come with me now."

"For what?" asked several people in the crowd in defense of the Sheriff and the others.

"Routine questioning," answered Agent Williams.

"Well," said the Sheriff. "You got me and Deputy Rory right here, but Aaliyah, Toby, and Cal were all transported to Providence already."

"The hospital?" asked Agent Williams.

"Yes," answered the Sheriff as the crowd became a bit agitated. The Sheriff tried to calm them down. He told them that there was an incident on the voyage, and the Mayor was no longer with them. This caused the crowd to gasp. Sheriff Jacoby told them that everything was going to be all right as he and Deputy Rory were ushered into the vehicle. The vehicles drove off, leaving the once joyful crowd in an absolute state of shock.

You see, although Bianca had reported the death of the Mayor in her live broadcast, it was one of the last things she reported. And the people in the crowd didn't stick around to hear the full report. They had made it to the beachfront as fast as they could, so the death of the Mayor was news to them all, and they all took it hard. As the crowd dispersed, Mrs. Li and Uncle Ken stared at Bianca as she and her camera crew " no longer rolling," loaded up into their news van and took off.

Bianca continued looking back at them until they were no longer in sight. A part of her questioned her own journalistic and moral ethics, knowing that her reporting the things she reported at the time she reported them would have the Sheriff and them tied up in scrutiny and unable to get the proper rest which they needed and also deserved. But this was good for Bianca's career. Bianca's got to look out for Bianca, right? I mean she doesn't make the news; she just report the news, right?

CHAPTER 10

THE PURCHASE

Well, my friends, I wish that I could say to you all that, in the end, everyone figured everything out and that all lived happily ever after, but that wasn't the case. Let's see, Cal died in the hospital from internal bleeding, but that's the short version. And here is the long version. Cal came into the hospital, suffering from prolonged hypothermia and excessive blood loss. This sent Cal into a comatose state, which in turn caused Cal to rapidly lose weight, which, unbeknownst to the doctors, this put excessive pressure on Cal's already cracked ribs, causing them to puncture his internal organs. Cal bled to death while they were treating an open cut across his forehead. Cal was in a coma for three weeks before he passed away.

A lot of people came to visit him, but Aaliyah and Toby came every day, and they were in the room with Cal when he was pronounced dead. Poor Toby. With Cal's passing, Toby officially was the last person alive in his family. This sent Toby into a downward spiral. Toby began to drink a lot, and his past time was self-loathing, and although he truly loved Aaliyah, his behavior caused him to neglect her and, at times, even treat her badly.

Aaliyah began to realize that this wasn't Toby mourning, this was Toby transforming into someone she didn't recognize. He would stay out late and sometimes not come home at all. Then Toby would get into fistfights, which, from the look of it, he would lose every time. Sheriff Rory (we'll get back to this later) brought Toby home after Toby had disturbed the peace, committed a lewd act, or started a fight and assaulted someone just for looking at the spectacle which he had become. With Sheriff Rory feeling pity for him, instead of taking him to jail, he would just drop him off at home, and the Sheriff would repeat the same thing every time, saying, "Don't let this happen again, Toby" or "I'm mo lock yo' butt up" "You have a good night now, Ms. Aaliyah." And Aaliyah would do her best to nurse Toby back from the brink of alcohol poisoning and tend to his wounds. But one day, Aaliyah had had enough. She bought herself a ticket to New York City and moved in with her mom, who, after the Mayor's memorial, had begged Aaliyah to come to New York and stay with her. But Aaliyah could not see herself separating from the love of her life, so she chose to stay with Toby, so she could be there for Toby. But now, her decision wasn't about Toby, it's about Aaliyah and what's best for Aaliyah. So one day, Toby woke up from one of his drunken episodes, and Aaliyah was gone. Sad, right?

But wait, there's more. Uncle Ken's daughter and son-in-law were both flying back from Malaysia, and their airplane went down. They both were assumed to be dead. It took a few months for Uncle Ken to receive word that their bodies were discovered floating in the Pacific Ocean, south of Japan. With this sad news, that meant that Uncle Ken now was the sole and full-time guardian of Amana and Jayce. But on a good note, this caused Uncle Ken and Mrs. Li to come out of the closet with their torrid love affair. They could no longer keep it from the kids. For weeks, Anne walked around town repeatedly exclaiming "I knew it!"

But this wasn't bad news at all. This was great news considering the circumstances. Now they all could be one big, happy family, but where would they stay? Neither Uncle Ken's nor Mrs. Li's home were nearly big enough for all six of them to share. Good thing Adam and Andy were awarded full custody of their jewels, all 110 pounds of them. Now it wasn't easy. After the investigation, their case went to court, and to make things worse, the museum got involved, stating that there were admiralty laws that governed treasures found at sea. This almost sealed it for Adam and Andy, but Sheriff Jacoby never gave up. He continued to work hard for the boys, looking for any way possible for them to keep their property. But Sheriff Jacoby was having no luck until on the very last day of the hearing. He got a call out of the blue, and you'll never guess from who. It was the one, the only Bianca Berkowitz, who had been richly rewarded for her bravery and hard-nosed reporting. She now had her own TV talk show and a massive fan base. She wrote a book called *The Adventures of Duck Poo Island*. It became a best seller and made it to Oprah's endorsement list. But she did not call to boast about her new-found fame and popularity. She called because she had found something that could help the boys' case. She told Sheriff Jacoby that maritime law states that an item found at that time unclaimed becomes the property of that finder's name. Seems pretty simple, right? Well, this little factoid won the boys their case. You see, Green Lake is a city in a maritime state. They take their pass-down ordinances very seriously. So, yes, the boys won their case, and to celebrate them winning their case, Adam and Andy performed the most amazing selfless act I have ever witnessed with my own two eyes. A class move. They donated ten pounds of the emeralds that they had just won to the very museum that fought tooth and nail for ownership of them. As they handed the 10 pounds of jewels to the curator of the museum, Adam and Andy, smiled and said, "No hard feelings."

The curator's and the judge's jaws dropped as the boys, being escorted by nearly the entire two towns, walked out of the courthouse and down Main Street while music composed by Beethoven played, and everyone cheered for their victors. By now, you all know what happened next—a party broke out. These two little towns like to party, and with these party being so plentiful, it seemed to bring the two towns together and created a bit of harmony that in the past years didn't seem to exist. Adam and Andy were good for Mallard County, two friends that swore to stay friends despite the odds.

So Andy was able to purchase his mom and Uncle Ken a very nice house, big enough for all six of them. Oh, and getting back to that Sheriff situation, Rory indeed became the new Sheriff, strongly because he was the right man for the job, but also because the position was open. And no, Sheriff Jacoby wasn't fired. He actually left his position and ran for Mayor unopposed. Did he win because the position was open? (May Mayor Meyers rest in peace.) No, he got the position of Mayor because he was the right man for the job.

Now some may see this as lobbying for political favors, but when Sheriff Jacoby became Mayor, that made it a lot easier for Adam and Andy to purchase the island and rename it Duck Poo Island. With the boys purchasing the island, they ran out of cash, so Uncle Ken, who Andy felt it would probably be best to call Ken since he was practically his stepfather now, offered to invest in their venture to help Adam and Andy accomplish their dream and vision. Also, other parties showed interest in the boy's business venture. How about you?

THE END

Lots of people want to ride with you in the limo, but what you want is someone who will take the bus with you when the limo breaks down.

—Oprah Winfrey

Ducks bombard the Island

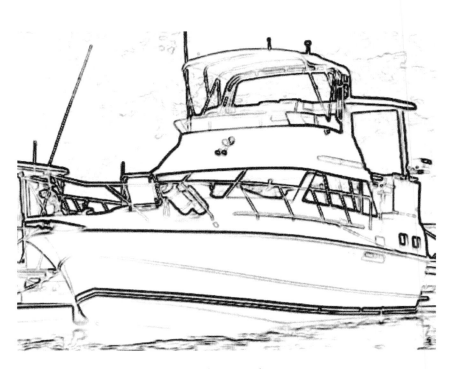

A yacht, people

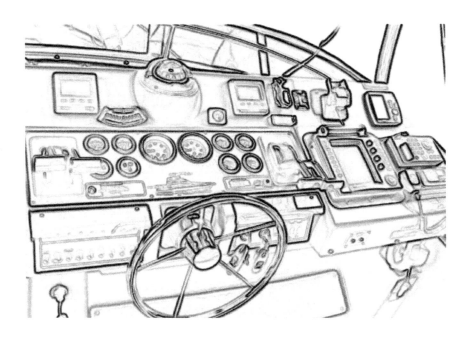

Very clean, immaculate even...

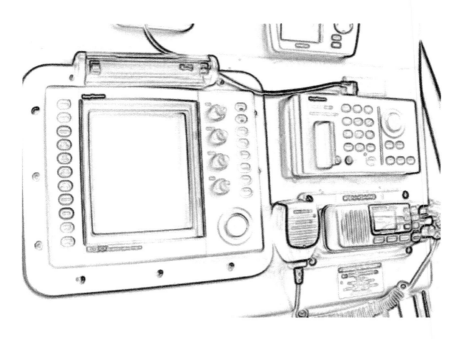

state-of -the-art nautical equipment...

loveseat for the steering wheel

ABOUT THE AUTHOR

Jizammie Griggs was born in Atlanta, Georgia to a single mom who lived in the projects, Eagen Homes, a social experiment of sorts. After ten year of surviving in the ghetto, Griggs' mom found the courage and strength to extract her children out of that guinea pig state of existence, and provide a life for them that offered many more options than just the ones they saw on a regular basis.

The author is convinced that with this single act his mom not only changed his life, but the lives of his entire family. For this reason, as well as many more, his mom, Alice M. Griggs, will be his hero until he dies. May God bless the process (by which Griggs means how we got here).

CPSIA information can be obtained at www.ICGtesting.com
Printed in the USA
BVOW08s0100240316

441445BV00002B/133/P